Pets Just Want to Have Fun!

Pets Just Want to Have Fun!

Written by Nicola Matthews
Illustrated by Eleanor Taylor

Hooked On Phonics®

Hooked On Phonics®

This version © 1998 Gateway Learning Corporation. The original work entitled, *Pets Just Want to Have Fun!*
Text Copyright © by Nicola Matthews 1998. Illustrations Copyright © by Eleanor Taylor 1998. Published by Bloomsbury Publishing Plc.
ISBN 1-887942-60-2
4 5 6 7 8 9 10

Contents

Contents

Special Words

Special words help make this story fun.
Your child may need help reading them.

Grandma

hose

pool

rope

sorry

tree

1. What Can We Do?

The sun is out, but Max has no one to play with. Polly is napping in the sun. She thinks it's too hot to play.

Mom is working in her flower beds. She does not want to play.

Max plays catch. But he is not good at it. He tosses the ball.

It zips up and lands with a crash in Mom's mug of tea.

"Oh, Max! That was not good! You spilled my tea and smashed my best mug. Why can't you play a different game?"

Max plays with his skates.
He spins very fast.

But he gets very wobbly, tips
over, and steps on Polly's tail.
Polly yelps and bumps into Mom.
Mom gets knocked over into the
flower beds.

"Max! Look out! Do not step on Polly's tail again! Why can't you play a different game?"

Max plays in the sandbox. He gets his trucks and begins to dig a track for them. He wants to make a big hill, but the sand needs to be wet.

He gets the hose, but just as he puts it on, Polly runs into him. The hose flips up and gets Mom all wet.

"Oh, Max!" says Mom.

But just then the bell rings. It is Jazz and Zug. Max is very glad to see them. It is much more fun to play catch with Jazz.

Polly can't nap in the sun with Zug there, so they play a game. Zug zips up with the hose. Polly runs past the flower beds, and Zug zips after her. He wants to get Polly wet with the hose, but Zug misses Polly.

He hits Mom, who has just put on a dry dress.

"I have a job for you. Why not go to the snack shop and get some snacks?" says Mom.

"Do not let the pets make problems, and be good!"

Mom gets Max money for the snacks. Then she rushes back into the house to get out of her wet dress—again.

"Have fun at the snack shop," says Mom. "We will," say Max and Jazz.

2. What Next?

Max, Jazz, Zug, and Polly set off
for the snack shop. On the way,
Max sees Pam and Jan jumping
rope. Max stops to chat. Polly
and Zug think jumping rope will
be fun.

But Zug has six legs, and
Polly is too big. They do not jump
very well.

Polly and Zug get all twisted up
in the rope.

Pam and Max and Jan and Jazz have to get them out of the rope. They are so mixed up that the jump rope snaps.

"Oh, no!" says Zug.

Pam and Jan are upset with
the pets. Jan just got that
jump rope.

"We will go with you and
tell your mom!" says Jan.

"But first we have to go to the snack shop," says Max.

On the way, they see Tom and Fred. Tom and Fred are playing soccer.

Max, Jazz, Pam, and Jan stop to chat. Polly and Zug want to play soccer too. Polly kicks the ball to Zug. Zug gets it and

chomps on it. There's a big hiss, and then the ball whizzes off. Dogs with claws and bugs with fangs are bad for soccer balls.

"Oh, no! Not again!" says Zug. Tom and Fred are mad at the pets. It's Fred's best soccer ball!

"We are going to tell Max's mom what they did to my jump rope," says Jan. "Why not come with us?"

But first they have to go to the
snack shop.

They pass a pool. Max sees Beth
standing by the pool. They stop to
chat. This is not a good thing to do.
What will the pets do next?

The pets jump into the pool and begin to play. The pool rips, and then the grass gets all wet. The pets get mud all over them.

Then Polly spots Fluff, the cat.
Polly begins to jump at Fluff.
Beth's mom and grandma come
out to see what the fuss is about.

Grandma does not like bugs!
She sees Zug and has to get up
the tree!

They all run after the pets.

Polly will not stop running after
the cat.

Fluff runs up in the tree with
Grandma. Fluff and Grandma
hang onto the tree trunk.

"Catch that cat!" yells Zug.

In the end, Jazz catches Zug and tucks him under her arm.

Max gets Polly and puts a rope on her. Beth is very upset with the pets.

"We need to go tell Max's mom what the pets did to us," says Tom. "Why not come too?"

But first Jazz, Max, Polly, Zug, Jan, Pam, Fred, Tom, and Beth have to go to the snack shop.

3. The Pets' Plan!

There are three shops in town—
a snack shop, a toy shop, and
a stamp shop. All the children go
into the snack shop. But they do
not let the pets come in. They
have mud all over them.

The pets can see into the toy
shop. They see a jump rope, a
soccer ball, and a pool!

Zug looks at Polly. "Why not?"
says Zug.

"Woof!" says Polly.

The pets slip into the toy shop.
Mister Bob does not see Zug
and Polly.

Polly grabs the jump rope.
Zug puts the soccer ball under his
wing. He grabs the pool with some
of his legs, and then he hops off.

That's when he bumps into a shelf. The shelf tips over with a crash. Mister Bob jumps up.

"What are you doing?" he yells.
"Oh, no! Polly! Run!" says Zug.
Polly runs out of the shop. Zug
runs after her as fast as he can.

Jazz and Max have gotten the
things Mom wanted. As they step
out of the snack shop, they see the

pets run off. They run after them.

All the children run with Jazz and Max. Mister Bob runs after them yelling, "Stop the pets!"

Mom is just getting back to her flower beds when Polly and Zug run in.

After them come Jazz, Max, Jan, Pam, Fred, Tom, Beth, and Mister Bob. They all look hot and mad.

"Now what?" says Mom.

4. Can We Fix This?

"Mom, I am sorry," says Max.

"I am very sorry too," says Jazz.

"That bug and that dog snapped my jump rope," says Jan.

"And popped my soccer ball,"
says Fred.

"And ripped my pool," says Beth.

"Your pets ran off with my toys,"
says Mister Bob.

They are all yelling at Polly
and Zug.

"Oh, no!" says Zug.

"Woof!" says Polly.

Mom wants to know what they all have to say. Max and Jazz are very upset. Mister Bob and all the children are upset.

"Stop! Stop!" says Mom.
"Let's not rush. You'll see.
We can fix this."

She gets the snacks from Max
and Jazz and makes a big picnic
with muffins and jam. Even
Mister Bob has some. Then they
all tell what happened.

"Well," says Mom. "The pets did not want to snap the rope, or pop the soccer ball, or rip the pool."

"We just wanted to have fun."
says Zug.

"Woof!" says Polly.

"I think they wanted to help
and say sorry," says Mom.

Polly wags her tail to say, "Yes!
Sorry!"

Zug bends down. "Sorry!"
he says.

Zug tells Mister Bob, "We do
not have money in space. I did not
know we needed money to get
the toys."

Mister Bob wants to know all about space. He says the children can have the toys, but the pets must know that they cannot just snatch things that they want.

Jan and Pam are very glad they have a jump rope. Fred and Tom are very glad too—they have a soccer ball. Beth is glad too. She has her pool back.

Then Beth says, "But what about Grandma and Fluff? I bet they are still up the tree!"

Jazz says she will bring them
muffins and jam to say sorry.
Mom is glad, and she hugs them.

Polly just wants to nap in the sun. But what about Zug?

Zug sits down on a good spot and snacks on muffins and jam.

But he makes a big mess when he eats.

Mom will not be glad for long!